Jane Burton is a native of Oklahoma. She has lived in places like Arizona, Oregon, and Colorado. She is an especially gifted and talented individual. She loves nature and baking cookies. All her creativity came from her own personal experiences from a journey that she shared with her best friend and partner. She wants to share her fun and exciting adventures with you so that you are inspired to make your own journeys.

Tobey the Trailer and His Great Adventures

Tobey the Adventurous Trailer

Jane Burton

AUSTIN MACAULEY PUBLISHERS™

LONDON • CAMBRIDGE • NEW YORK • SHARJAH

Copyright © Jane Burton (2020)

Ordering Information:
Quantity sales: special discounts are available on quantity purchases by corporations, associations, and others. For details, contact the publisher at the address below.

Burton, Jane
Tobey the Trailer and His Great Adventures

ISBN 9781643788722 (Paperback)
ISBN 9781643788715 (Hardback)
ISBN 9781645365457 (epub e-book)

Library of Congress Control Number: 2019917028

www.austinmacauley.com/us

First Published (2020)
Austin Macauley Publishers LLC
40 Wall Street, 28th Floor
New York, NY 10005
USA

mail-usa@austinmacauley.com
+1 (646) 5125767

Dedicated to Bonnie Genzer, better known as AJ, who passed away on July 17, 2018, with whom I shared the journeys to tell. And my mom, who is on a different journey.

Hi! My name is Tobey the trailer. I'm for sale, because my family no longer needs me. I hope someone nice comes along to buy me so I can have fun again.

6

Oh! There's someone coming to my family's yard sale; maybe they will be nice people and be interested in taking me along with them, **thought** Tobey to himself. Oh, how great it would be to be loved once again.

YIPPEE, YAY, YAY! They decided to buy me and take me with them. I wonder where I'll be going soon—I can't wait to be behind them— it's going to be so exciting, thought Tobey.

Here we go, how exciting! I would jump up and down if I could, but I'm sure the road will do enough of that for me. "**Hello**, my name is **Black**. I'm going to be pulling you, so try not to ride my butt too hard," said Black. *What did he mean by that?* thought Tobey.

"What kind of adventure are we going on, Black?" asked Tobey.
"I do believe you have become a home to them two girls. What they
have planned for you I'm not sure," said Black. "I'm a 1958," said
Tobey. "What year are you, Black?"
"I'm a 1977, you're an old man. You do realize it's 1994?"
asked Black.
"I feel young at heart, ha-ha," said Tobey.

"Here is your new temporary parking space," said Black.
"Wow! I can see the river and the boats coming and going, this sure
beats that hill," said Tobey.
"Well, I'm off to work now, we'll see you tonight," said Black.
"Do you know what town we're in?" asked Tobey.
"I do believe we are in the town of Walport, Oregon," said Black.

"Wow! This is so cool," said Tobey. "Hi, Mr. RV! Hi,
Mr. Tugs (for tugboat)!"
"Toot-Toot," said Mr. Tugs.
"Why are you here?" asked Mr. RV. "You look like a camping trailer."
"I became them girls' new home, and I'm proud," said Tobey.

12

Black arrived home that evening. *I am so glad to see they are back,* thought Tobey. "Black, how long have you been with them girls?" asked Tobey.
"Well, they found me on the seaside a couple of weeks ago, rusting out from the salt from the ocean and adopted me like they adopted you," said Black.

The next day came, overcast—probably going to rain. *With the fog so thick right now, I can't see 2 ft in front of me. This is going to be a real entertaining day; I can't wait until Black comes home. I wish Mr. RV would pack up and go. He acts really grumpy; I guess because it takes all his energy to haul his weight,* Tobey thought.

It has been a quiet day, looks like a storm brewing, thought Tobey. *I do hope they arrive soon, looks like a cold spell also. Sometimes, it's rather lonely. Oh well! It's all going to be great.*

Here comes Black around the corner, I can barely see him because it's so dark tonight. Oh wow! He's all loaded with goodies, thought Tobey to himself. "What's the goodies for, Black?" asked Tobey.
"They're for the inside of you so they can make you feel like a home," said Black.

14

I can't wait to see what they do, and what kind of goodies they are, thought Tobey. "Tell me, Black, I can't see what they are putting inside me." Black described several things: some things to cook, eat, heat, and feel just at home. They all felt so cozy, and then the rain came.

The rain came for several days; the girls came and went for several days. Some days, it seemed forever until they came home; then others, they were hardly gone at all. It seemed like weeks had gone by because rain seemed to keep you in the dark.

One evening when Black arrived home, he had a real concerned and worried face. Tobey asked, "What's wrong, Black?"
He said, "This doesn't concern you quite yet, Tobey, so don't worry your little head. I'll give you some heads up, don't worry, just be happy, Tobey."

16

When Black arrived home that evening, Tobey asked Black how his day was and whether he would mind telling him about where they were working.
Black started describing to Tobey what the home looked like and all its surroundings that one could see near and far.

Black stated that it was a beautiful 3-storey Victorian style home that sat right on the cliff overlooking the ocean, that one could see at least 100 miles out into the ocean and how the river joined the ocean. It seemed so beautiful.

That evening, the rain had cleared off a little bit. *Maybe we'll have some sunshine soon,* thought Tobey. The girls built a campfire, they played music, and everyone seemed to be enjoying themselves quite freely.

The next morning, Tobey overheard a conversation that the girls were having and they said they might be leaving soon. *Right before Black leaves, I'll just mention it to him; seems like he is sleeping right now and I'm not about to wake him so he might bite my head off. No way, no how!* thought Tobey to himself.

"Let me holler at you real quick," Tobey said to Black, "I overheard a conversation this morning when you were still asleep. Are we leaving soon, Black, going on a new adventure, huh, Black?"
"Boy, you sure keep talking. I told you to bother none. Time will be soon. I'm sure," said Black.

The next few days came and went, the rain had stopped. All of a sudden, Black said, "It's time to go now, boy. I hope you hold up on the open road and don't fall apart on me, like we're driving down the road and, all of a sudden, all four walls pop off, **HA-HA!**" *Boy, I can't figure out if I should take him seriously,* thought Tobey.

20

The girls had them packed and hooked up to Black within the hour. So Tobey assumed they were about ready to pull out. Tobey thought he had better say all his goodbyes which weren't too many; it was almost October and they didn't seem to have too much going on. In this part of the country, it's super busy during the spring and summer only.

22

As they were pulling out, Tobey got to say "See you" to Mr. Tugs,
"Thanks for the great company."
"Goodbye, Tobey, have a safe trip," said Mr. Tugs.
"Black, do you know where we are going?" asked Tobey. "No, I just
feel the stretch of road in front of me," said Black.
"Hang on and feel the ride!"

24

Tobey said, "I am getting ready to set on a new adventure and new horizons. This is so exciting; I can hardly wait." The adventure of Tobey the trailer continues…

www.ingramcontent.com/pod-product-compliance
Lightning Source LLC
Chambersburg PA
CBHW082225140626
46556CB00019B/3309